Murder on the Eiffel Tower

Brie Kraus

For any who have ever had excitement in Paris.

Murder on the Eiffel Tower

Chapter 1

As the crowds came rushing through the airport, my parents and I just stood there, amazed by this beautiful sight. There were many couples together, and many families with their excited children ready to go to Disneyland. This was truly the place to be, I thought. I had never experienced such a happy atmosphere in one place. It was the perfect way to relax, following the tragic events of the previous weeks. We (or my parents) had chosen to fly here instead of getting the ferry because my father insisted that it would be much easier to do so, than get into a car, drive all the way to Dover, get on the ferry, and drive through half of France. The expenses of that would have meant that the flight would not have cost much more anyway; so there we were, stood at the airport in Paris, waiting for our taxi to take us to the hotel.

"Now, promise me you're going to relax," my mother asked me, anxious about how I was feeling.

"You've asked that about six times already, Fallon," my father said to my mother.

This was their first holiday together ever since my grandmother was murdered. My mother seemed to forget about the whole thing now and move on with her life. After all, it had been four years.

"Well, Tammy has experienced a lot of stress these past few years, Joe," my mother kept saying to my father quietly, "and this last case just topped it all off!"

"I promise you I will forget about Barry Scott!" I emphasized. I did truly want to forget about the whole case back at home; that was one of the main reasons for spending five days in France. Mitchell saw the stress I was going through, and suggested that I take a break for a few days. I reluctantly agreed. So I was here, at the airport, waiting for the taxi to take us to the hotel. I had to agree, I was beginning to become obsessed with catching Barry Scott for what he did, but I knew I needed to forget, and Paris was the place to make me forget.

And ever since I broke up with Danny (again), I had to come to Paris by myself. I told him I was prepared to take him back, to see if we could sort out our worries and problems, but after a couple of weeks, I decided to give up, as he did not seem to appreciate me. I told him that we could take things slowly, although deep down, I did not think that we could get back together again after what had happened, but I still cared about him, and I could not deny that at all. So there I was, standing in the airport with my parents, waiting for the taxi to take us to the hotel.

The taxi did arrive after a few minutes.

"Here it is!" cried dad, hugging mum and half-jumping around. I just put my case into the boot of the car and jumped in without a fuss. Clearly, my parents were more excited about this trip than me, even though I was looking forward to it. We were told that the hotel itself was not in the center of Paris - it was on the outskirts, so I was quite relieved and disappointed at the same time - I could relax properly, but I wanted to get into the city center easily to see all of the sights, but I knew that problem could be solved.

Whilst we were loading the bags into the car and whatever else, I heard a heated conversation behind us. I could hardly make out what they were saying, so I turned around to look at them.

"Just shut up with your snide comments" cried the woman, "there's no point in trying to deny it now, Christopher!"

"Then why don't you just divorce me, you stupid woman?"

The woman gave the man a sly look. "I'm not going to let you get away that easily! I'm never going to divorce you, so when you die first, and you will because you are significantly older than me, I will be able to take all of your money and your businesses!"

The woman laughed out loud. I assumed that she had found out about an affair the man had been having, so I did not know whether to empathize with her or dislike her for her childish behavior.

Despite the blazing hot weather, the woman wore a fur coat and the man wore business-like clothes, so I deduced that they were of a higher class. I did not want to look that much into it, because I was concentrating more on going on holiday.

We were sat in the taxi, seeing the sights of France, and the radio was turned on. I could not believe how fast the French could speak! Neither my parents nor I could speak a word of French apart from "bonjour," so we struggled with it. Unfortunately, the taxi driver rambled on in French. I think he asked us if we had been to France before, because I heard the words, "a France" and he sounded like he was asking a question, from his tone of voice. I just said, "non," and my parents looked very confused.

"Ah," said the driver, "c'est assez dangereuse, mais c'est tres reposante et incroyablement beau!"

I only understood one word in that sentence: dangerous.

We arrived at the hotel, and it was the most stunning place I had ever been to! There were plants growing from the sides of the walls, and a miniature waterfall on each side of the gate. A young female servant came to the gates to greet us, and she helped with the luggage.

"Bonjour, et bienvenue a l'Hotel du Soleil!" she said.

We all looked at her, as if to say, "we don't know any other word than 'bonjour'."

"Oh, sorry," the servant replied, "hello, and welcome to the Sunshine Hotel!"

That was quite a simple name, I thought, but it did not matter. This place was clearly the best hotel I had ever stayed in, and I could not wait to get inside and start my adventure.

Chapter 2

"I know now that this is going to be a great holiday!" my mother cried, hugging her husband, "I just wish we went away before now!"

"I can't wait to get started!" cried my father, almost dragging his suitcase inside.

When we walked inside, the ambience stunned us. In the background, beautiful slow music played, and the whole room was spotless. The stairs were made of marble, and they shone from the glittering lights that hung from the white ceiling. It was like been in Heaven. Everywhere I looked was either white or near to that: this was the place to be for a holiday.

At the reception, we noticed a nervous looking woman, waving us over.

"Hello," she said, "I'm Chloe, and I'm the manager of the Sunshine Hotel."

The manager was quite tall, had short, curly hair and a long, thin nose. She seemed unconfident for a manager, but that may have been due to stress.

"This is a lovely place!" my mother expressed, knowing that this was probably the best place she had ever been to.

"You're too kind!" said Chloe, rubbing her hands together. "Now, we need to see your passports before we check you in, just so we know who you are."

My parents and I showed Chloe the passports.

"Right then," said this seemingly friendly woman, "we'll have your room ready in about ten minutes. For now, why don't you sit on the balcony with the rest of the guests; it's a lovely day."

So, we were ready to begin our holiday. We took the bags. Before I left the room to go to the balcony, I heard Chloe speak to one of the members of the staff: "Adrienne. Allez a la cuisine et donnez lui des boissons. Maintenant!"

I did not know what she said, but she seemed quite aggressive. Perhaps Chloe was not as nice as I thought she was, I thought.

Anyway, we walked outside on to the balcony, which showed us a view of the beautiful French countryside. I looked out for the Eiffel Tower, but no such luck, yet. I was looking forward to climbing it, and seeing Paris from the top. I knew that my time would come.

There were other guests sitting around the balcony, drinking glasses of various types of alcohol. Three couples one newlyweds, one middle-aged, and the third quite old) sat in lounge chairs staring at us.

"Hello," said the elderly man.

"Hello," I said, taking a seat right in the middle of them all.

"Anyway, as I was saying," said the fairly young woman, "we were quite surprised to see you here, Stephanie. You never said you were going!"

"Well, it was to celebrate out engagement," replied the young woman, holding the hand of the man next to her.

"After the wedding, we are going to Tenerife, but we just thought we'd have a romantic stay in Paris, first," added the young man.

"How long is it now?" asked the other man. I saw a wedding ring on his finger, so it was obvious that he was married to the woman sat next to him, although anybody could deduce that.

"Four months," replied Stephanie, almost jumping up and down with excitement. "I still can't believe it when I say that!"

"We've been married for ten years, haven't we, Alan?" said the woman.

"Yes. Shona and I came here because of our anniversary. Even though we had a party, I wanted more for it, just to celebrate a little more," said Alan, giving his wife a kiss.

I looked at the married couple. I thought it was unusual, because looking at them, you would not think that they were able to afford a luxury holiday and a party at the same time, just for one special occasion.

"Well, this is certainly the place to be!" replied the old woman. "Frank and I have been coming here for almost thirty years, and we still love it!"

"Really?" said Shona.

"Yes. Paris is literally the city of love."

"How long have you been married?" asked Brendan, the one who was engaged to Stephanie.

"Sixty-one years," the old man replied with pride.

There were gasps all around. It was amazing to see such happiness in the atmosphere. I had never had that much. Instead, I was stressed out and could not even afford to go on holiday, but the hotel introduced a special offer, and we were fortunate enough to be the first to get a place.

I then noticed that, apart from Brendan and Stephanie, who were about to get married, I was the only one here who was not married, or with anybody. That made me slightly depressed, but I shook it off, determined to enjoy myself.

Then, the servant who Chloe yelled at came in with some drinks.

"Your...drinks," he said, with a broken accent.

Whilst this conversation about love and happiness was going on, I heard voices in the background. I was stunned when I turned around and saw that those voices were those of the same two people who were arguing at the airport!

"Oh, hello, Veronica," said Chloe, with a bitter tone of voice.

"Chloe, my old friend!" cried Veronica, clearly sarcastic.

"How are you these days?" asked Chloe.

"Still as happy as ever," Veronica said, unconvincingly.

"So, are we going to get checked in or what?" said the man.

"Yes, Christopher," replied Chloe.

"We want the best service in this hotel!" cried Veronica.

"Well, you've come to the right place," said Chloe, trying not to be over-dramatic.

Chloe checked them in, and told them that their rooms were ready.

"So, later this evening, are we having cocktails?" said Christopher, rubbing the palm of his hand against the back of hers.

Chloe moved her hands away from his. "As we always do," she replied, swallowing the lump in her throat.

"Oh, that's fantastic," said Christopher, winking at Chloe.

Veronica laughed it off just to hide the embarrassment, if there was any. They walked upstairs in silence, and that was that.

"I hate that bitch!" cried Stephanie.

"So do I," said Shona, "I can't believe she's here."

Chloe was listening to our conversation.

"How do you know her?" I asked them.

"Over the years, she's done all sorts of things," Alan said.

"Like what?" my mother asked.

"Well, she lives in the town we live in, in that big, fancy house. Anyway, years ago, she got pregnant to this wealthy man, and she blackmailed him, telling him that if he did not give her any money, she would terminate the child. Anyway, she did have the termination in the end, even though she pretended that she was pregnant, still. So, he was paying her money, and by the time she was five or six months gone, she said that he could have the child. She carried on pretending to be pregnant by carrying a watermelon in her stomach. That man was now with another woman, and she was jealous of that, because he had previously dated her. Anyway, Veronica did not reveal her lies until she pretended to go into labour, right in front of this man's eyes, and she threw the watermelon out of her shirt. He's never been the same since!"

"She sounds insane!" cried the elderly woman.

"She is. I could go on all day, telling you stories, but I don't want to ruin the atmosphere," said Alan.

I then looked up, and saw a window open. I wondered if it was actually their window that was open, because I did not think that it was open before. If so, then it would be awkward the next time we saw Veronica.

"Right, everybody," said Chloe, dashing into the seating area, "I have two good things to tell you. First, your rooms are ready, and secondly, I've booked a trip into Paris for tomorrow, if anybody wants to come!"

There were cheers of excitement in the air. It was official: everybody there was going to Paris.

Chapter 3

After having finished unpacking, we realized that it nighttime approached and were surprised at how time had moved so fast; although, we soon realized that France was an hour ahead, so, to us, it would seem like that.

Earlier that day, Chloe had invited us down for some cocktails, free of charge, as a complimentary drink for choosing to go to her hotel. It seemed to me that she was desperate, but I did not care, nor did I care to drink alcohol, as I had neither the time nor the interest to consume it, but I knew that in this instance, I was defeated. I had to let my hair down at some point.

We dressed in slacks and skirts for the occasion, since we assumed that everybody in the hotel would be down for these complimentary drinks as it was a small hotel. If I had to estimate at how many rooms there were, I would say twenty. Chloe had obviously worked very hard to get here. For its size, I assumed that the hotel would not get much revenue compared to the costs of maintenance, which made me interested. Perhaps Chloe had future plans.

We arrived down the stairs, and, to our surprise, hardly anybody was there. The Sandersons (Alan and Shona) and Stephanie and Brendan were, but no one else.

"Hello," said Chloe, rushing over to us like an excited terrier dog. "I hope you have enjoyed your stay here so far!"

"We have," my parents replied.

"That's fantastic news! Other people should be down shortly, but please, take a cocktail each."

"What's in it?" I asked Chloe, taking a cocktail from the bar.

"Well, it is made of absinthe and champagne. The name of it is Death in the Afternoon."

"That's an unusual name for a cocktail," I said.

"Isn't it just?" said Chloe.

I didn't know why, but she gave me some sort of twitch when she said that—reminiscent of Norman Bates from Psycho, which made me think that she was planning a murder, but then I remembered that not everybody in the world is a psychopath.

"So," my father said, trying to converse with Alan, "where are you actually from?"

"Well, we're living in Manchester now, but we're not originally from there," said Alan. "We used to live in Lanchester—both of us."

"Ah," said my father, as if he were a detective.

The Dewells arrived, changing the casual, relaxed atmosphere of laughs and jokes; when they entered the room, no one spoke a word. The Sandersons and Brendan and Stephanie looked at Veronica, as did Chloe. Somehow, Veronica reminded me of one of the murder victims in a previous case of mine; she was arrogant, loved showing off, and bitchy. She had many enemies. Nobody in the building liked her. I had not even spoken to her, but I knew exactly what she was. I began to feel sorry for Christopher, and started to think that he had a justifiable reason for cheating on his wife.

Veronica approached Chloe.

"What the Hell is this?" she said, her fingers grasping the glass.

"This is called Death in the Afternoon," said Chloe.

"Well, I've never tried this one before," said Veronica, taking the glass and sipping it. She put it back on the tray and said, "I don't like it. I want another cocktail."

Chloe turned round to her female servant.

"Allez a la cuisine et donnez lui du vin pas cher."

I tried to translate that in my head: go to the kitchen and give them some wine., or something like that. I recognized some of the words because Chloe had said them before when we first entered the hotel.

The female servant reappeared with some new wine.

"What on Earth is this?" said Vera.

"It's something you'd like," said Chloe, trying not to be too smug.

"This is probably the cheapest wine on the market!" she yelled.

"Well, Death in the Afternoon is one of the most expensive cocktails on the market, so I thought you'd like the opposite."

Even though she was vile, I still would not treat Veronica like that if she were my guest. She just turned around and walked over to the piano, muttering, "When I get home I'm going on Trip Advisor to write a bad review of this place!"

Then something startled even me. Christopher sat down at the grand piano, with Veronica next to him. He pressed a few keys, and Veronica started to sing.

You're the top, you're the coliseum.
You're the top, you're the Louvre Museum.
You're the melody from a symphony by Strauss.
You're a vandal bonnet, a Shakespeare sonnet,
you're Mickey Mouse!
You're the Nile, you're the Tower of Pisa,
You're the smile on the Mona Lisa.
I'm a worthless cheque, a total wreck, a flop.
But if babe I'm the bottom, you're the top!

This woman was clearly the biggest show off I had ever seen. She had attracted the attention of everybody in the room, and worst of all, she could not sing, sounding more like a screeching cat with a bad case of emphysema. She started making up her own lyrics for the song:

You're the top of the Eiffel Tower.
You're the top, you're the finest hour!
You're the boat I like on the lovely River Seine.
If you were Champs Elyseees, I'd like to say I'd
come again!
You're the top, you're the Pont Alexandre,
you're the wine, with a snail-filled dinner.
I'm the frog without a leg on which to hop.
But if babe I'm the bottom, you're the top!"

Veronica stopped singing, and bowed down. Many of the other guests clapped, including some members of staff clapped, except Chloe, applauded as well. Veronica loved the attention, which proved my deduction of her earlier on.

Chloe approached me, and said, "If you want a fantastic view of the countryside, go outside in the back where the swimming pool is. You can see for miles around!"

It was not completely dark yet, although the Sun had set. I decided to catch a quick view of the countryside; I wasn't one for socializing anyway.

I went outside, and Chloe was right; the view was absolutely stunning and breathtaking. So this was what it was like to see the world, and tomorrow, I would see the whole of Paris. I was very excited about it.

Suddenly, although he did not notice me, I spied Christopher Dewell sneaking off. He went behind the back of the building, literally tiptoeing so he did not make any noise. I followed him, to see what he was up to.

"I've waited so long to see you," said a woman's voice.

"Did the others see us?" he said.

"No. I made sure of it."

Silence followed as they sunk themselves into a passionate kiss. I then joked to myself: it was Paris, after all, until my curiosity about who this mystery woman was took hold. I knew it was too much of a risk to peek around the corner. Could it be Shona, or Stephanie, or even Chloe? I thought it might be Chloe.

Anyway, I decided to sneak back into the hotel before they caught m. It was ironic because they were the ones who were supposed to be secretly doing something, but I did not want to get involved. I went back inside and acted as though nothing had happened, not feeling sorry for Veronica one bit.

It had been a long day, so we all decided it was time to go to bed, for tomorrow was going to be a big day.

That night, in my stifling room, I opened the window only to be inundated with the argument in full force in the room next door, which I heard Alan and Shona Sanderson going into before.

"Why did you have to get involved with him again?" Alan said.

"How many times do I have to tell you, Alan? I did not get involved with him!"

"Then where did you go when he went outside for a cigarette?"

"I told you. I went outside to look at the view!"

"You're lying!"

"Prove it!"

"Alright, I will," said Alan. "I'll go and ask that Tammy tomorrow, shall I? She was outside when you were, so let's see what she has to say!"

My fears had come true; I did not want to get involved in it, but if Shona was having an affair, then perhaps Alan should know the truth. However, I just thought about the ten years of marriage, and that marriage was now in my hands.

Chapter 4

Throughout the night, I lay awake, thinking about the next day. Ever since I was a small girl, I wanted to go to Paris and see the Eiffel Tower, and today was going to be the day. I had never had time to go on holidays, nor did my parents, having been too busy taking care of more important matters over the years.

The morning eventually arrived, and surprisingly, I was not tired. I put on a summer dress, judging by the images on weather station it seemed to indicate that it would be a nice day, even though I did not understand a word they said. It was early in the morning, but at least we would have the full day in the city. Chloe said that it would take about half an hour to get to the city center, which was not bad, considering Paris was a capital city, and we were on the outskirts.

When I got downstairs, I was surprised to see that almost everybody who was going on the trip was there: the Sandersons, Stephanie and Brendan, and of course, the Dewells, although they were not with the others in the red outdoor seating area, but out of the way on a nearby table. Chloe then arrived, looking as stressed as ever.

"Right, everyone," she said, "the bus will leave in ten minutes. Now, where are those Miltons?"

No answered.

"If they don't hurry up we'll have to leave without them!" Chloe cried, pulling her hair.

"They'll get here," said Veronica, "don't worry."

"Oh," said Stephanie, "I've forgotten my sun cream! I'll just be a minute."

"You were looking for it earlier, weren't you?" said Brendan.

"Yes. I don't know where it is," replied Stephanie.

"I'll help you look for it," I offered, considering I had nothing else to do. Stephanie agreed, so we went up the stairs and on to the first floor, directly above the outdoor seating area.

"It's a lovely place, isn't it?" she said.

"It's one of the most beautiful places I've ever been to," I replied, still feeling as though I was living a dream.

Stephanie went out on to the balcony, where she saw the bottle of sun cream. Before picking it up, she took her dry red towel from the rail, and put a wet, blue towel over the balcony, leaving the green one in the shade.

"I'll have to leave this one in the shade," she said, pointing to the green one, "because this one tends to fall off and fall into the seating area."

Stephanie and I continued to make small talk. She seemed like a very nice girl, and I was happy for her that she was engaged. That reminded me of Alan and Shona.

We got downstairs, and found the others were now by the swimming pool, including Veronica.

"It's nicer here," said Shona, "we get more Sun."

Alan, Shona, Brendan all talking to Veronica, and I found that rather strange. Then again, she might have been nice to talk to if she did not dislike you. I wondered if I wanted to approach her to start a conversation with her, but then again, I decided to go out and look for my parents.

"Those bloody Miltons!" cried Chloe, "we've only got five minutes before we leave!"

"They'll get here," said my father, trying to calm Chloe down.

"I knew this would happen. I knew it would! Every week, we go into Paris, and nothing ever changes. Somebody either takes ill, or there is some sort of drama!"

"Calm down!," said my mother, becoming stressed for no apparent reason.

I noticed Christopher on his own, doing nothing but sat in the sunshine in the red seating area.

Fortunately, the Miltons arrived, dawdling down the stairs.

"Good morning, Mr. and Mrs. Milton," Chloe said, altering her tone from irate to sweet. "Did you sleep well?"

25

"Yes," said Mr. Milton, "very well. We aren't late, are we?"

"No. Of course not!," cried Chloe.

Now that everybody had arrived, we all got on to the to the minibus, ready for our exciting adventure into the depths of the city of love.

Chapter 5

There was one word to describe the main part of Paris: magnificent. It was the most beautiful place I had ever been to. The buildings just blew me away; their innate structure displayed the true characteristic of the French, making me eager to see more. I loved every single atom in Paris that existed at that moment in time; I truly believed I was in Heaven. Everybody else around me loved it as well, except for Chloe, of course, who was too busy stressing out about the schedule for the day. We had been in the bus for five minutes when Chloe picked up a microphone and started to speak.

"Good morning everybody," she said "It's usually a larger group than this, but never mind. It's easier with just a few people, anyway. Today, we are going to see the main sights of Paris. Now, first, we are going to go on a boat trip. It's a little unusual during the day, but less people are present, and it's just as nice anyway..."

I detested the way in which Chloe expressed her opinions as facts. It would have been much nicer when it was dark.

"..when we are on the boat, we will pass some monuments: some famous bridges, the Notre Dame Cathedral, and of course, the Eiffel Tower. We will then go off into the town for some dinner, before going to the Eiffel Tower itself!"

Cheers rose up, filling the bus. I was even tempted to join in. This was going to be the perfect day; I knew it.

As Chloe said, the first thing that we did was go on the boat trip. I enjoyed it, even though I would have preferred to have gone on it at night. The boat meandered through the water, allowing us to engross ourselves in the sights of the most romantic city in the world.

On the boat, my parents and I sat near the front, while Stephanie, Brendan, and the Sandersons were behind us; the Dewells were sat out of the way, with the Miltons in the seat next to them in their own state of bliss as they marveled at the peace surrounding them, away from the crowd on the boat.

"Do you mind if I take a photo?" asked Stephanie, seeing that I had a camera in my hand. "I'm interested in photography."

"Of course," I said, passing her the camera.

While Stephanie took the photo, Veronica surprised me again by conversing with the Miltons and Chloe. Before, she had shown no interest in the

Miltons (or Chloe for that matter) but now, she was keen to talk to them.

"So, what other exciting adventures are we getting up to this week?" said Vera.

"Well, on Thursday, I'm arranging a visit into the little French village next to our hotel," said Chloe, attracting the attention of the neighbor. "It's a nice place. A lot of things that happened in the war stayed there, and it's interesting to see what the people from World War One left for us."

"Sounds interesting," said Veronica, smiling.

Christopher listened in, while the rest of the group ignored it.

To my great and utter astonishment, when I turned round, underneath the empty seat next to me, I saw a gun—a pistol!

"That was not there before!" I cried. "How on Earth did this get here?"

Everybody on the boat just sat in silence, staring as we approached the Notre Dame.

"Somebody has just put this gun here!" I cried.

"Well...we'll hand it to the police," said Chloe, acting a bit nervous and shaky.

I wondered who could have put the gun there. Perhaps somebody on the boat dropped it when they walked past?

Although everybody were still a bit agitated, they continued to take photographs, torn between the mystery of the gun and the wonderment of the Cathedral.

"Let's just try to forget about this," said Chloe with a nervous chuckle.

I could not help being suspicious, but decided to leave it alone since I was on vacation and did not wish to get involved.

After having wandered around the city, we visited a fancy restaurant for dinner. I was keen to try the French cuisine, although I decided to give the snails a miss.

Dinner was nice, but I was still saddened to see the destroyed relationship between Alan and Shona. Because they whispered and sat on a separate table away from the rest of the group, I could not make out what they were saying, but their animated movements made it plain that they were arguing.

In contrast, Stephanie and Brendan loved every minute of dinner. It was a traditional romantic meal in Paris: they shared spaghetti, and, mimicking *Lady And The Tramp*, they got hold of one piece, slurped it together, and reached the end, which resulted in a kiss. Personally, I thought that it was a bit overdramatic, but they were on holiday, in Paris, and young lovers. Stephanie and Brendan laughed and joked, taking photos on their mobile phones, standing against the window, which showed the Eiffel Tower in the background.

I looked at the Dewells: I did not know what to make of them. They just did not speak. They looked in opposite directions, like they had been told some devastating news or something. On occasion, each would take a sip of their soup, or a bite of their baguette.

Bored with them, I looked at the Miltons. Again, it was nice to see romance, both young and old. The Miltons were happy together, and had been all their lives They ate escargot, the very dish that disgusted me and made me want to vomit. Once finished, they got up and looked out of the window, watching life go by in one of the most stunning capital cities of the world.

When everybody had finished their dinner, Chloe said, "If everybody is ready to proceed, we shall, and the next stop is the Eiffel Tower!"

Again, cheers and claps rang out, as we headed for what was possibly the most amazing experience of our lives: the Eiffel Tower.

Chapter 6

My skin tingled from my head to the tips of my toes as we approached the Eiffel Tower. This was the moment I had been waiting for. Ever since I was a young girl, I had wanted to visit it, and now that I was here, standing right next to it, it was like my dream had come true. It made me forget about the horrible event that had occurred at home; all of my anger and self-hatred had gone. I now felt more confident within myself again, and I looked forward to enjoying life again, putting that brief period of depression behind me.

Chloe got all of the tickets for us, and it was announced that we would have to take the stairs up to the second floor, because the lifts were far too busy and the queues were too long. Although there were several groans behind me, I would have preferred to walk it anyway; it was part of the experience, realized that the Miltons would have to walk up with us.

"I'll help escort you up," I offered them.

"Why, thank you, young lady," said Doreen Milton.

"I can do that," said Chloe, grabbing Frank Milton by the arm.

"I can come with you, anyway," I argued, "I would prefer to walk slowly anyway."

"Well, if you insist," said Chloe, looking somewhat disappointed.

The others dashed up the tower, including my parents, who left me behind. I just waited with the Miltons and Chloe. On the way up, I glanced through the iron bars, and kept looking down. It was a huge drop, and it gradually got bigger as we walked up each flight of stairs. I loved every minute of it, though. I was on the Eiffel Tower!

I kept touching the bars, just so I could touch the Eiffel Tower and noticed that the tower had an unusual structure to it; from where I stood, it seemed that each bar went off in the opposite direction to the one next to it. I could see right through some of the gaps at times, right to the other side. It was fantastic.

"Are you alright?" Chloe said to Doreen, who walked slower and slower.

"Perhaps we could have a five minute break on the first floor?" replied Doreen, out of breath.

"Of course," said Chloe, giving a huge grin.

"So have you sorted out that business with the gun?" asked Frank.

"We're just going to forget about that," said Chloe, moving her hand in such a way that it resembled her shoving something out of the way, like a person.

We reached the first floor.

"You can go and catch up with the others if you like," said Chloe. "They're not that far ahead. I can see them from here."

I did not want to leave Mrs. Milton, but Chloe's insistence persuaded me to. By the time I reached the second floor, I was exhausted, which was worrying for a woman of my age. I was elated when I saw that there was a big queue for the refreshments.

"Here you are, honey," my mother said, saving the day by handing me a bottle of water. I was so grateful at that moment in time.

I went over to the ledge, where I stood next to Stephanie and Brendan.

"It's lovely, isn't it?" said Stephanie.

"It's the most beautiful thing I've ever seen," was my reply and went around the second floor, taking a few photos.

After having finished snapping pictures, I walked back to the queue for refreshments to see if the line had shortened; I was quite hungry. Unfortunately, it was still busy. Instead, I decided to explore the tower a little more and saw that Veronica was not with Christopher (although that was not a surprise). He was on his own, where nobody else was around, taking photos, while Veronica was on a different side of the tower, doing the same.

Stephanie screamed. "Oh my God!"

Brendan, Alan, and Shona surrounded her, confused by her hysterical behavior.

"What's the matter?" asked Alan.

"I dropped my ice cream over the ledge!" she cried, "and now it's going to land on somebody's head!"

"Oh my God!" cried Shona.

"Now, a person at the bottom is going to get the fright of their life!"

Stephanie broke down. I thought it was a bit too dramatic, but then again, I had seen Stephanie being overly dramatic before.

Suddenly, I got another fright when I heard a loud bang!

It came from the other side of the tower. When we all got there, we were astounded to see that Christopher Dewell had been shot in the head!

"He's dead!" screamed Veronica.

I knew that that was true. Now, everybody, including Chloe and the Miltons, surrounded Christopher's dead body. Just then, another shot rang out, but this time, it came from the other side of the tower. We all ran towards it, but found no one.

"I can't believe this has happened!" screamed Chloe.

Doreen Milton fainted. Stephanie continued to cry, collapsing to the floor, shaking like a baby. Veronica just stood there, looking over a ledge of the tower. I could not make out her facial expression, but one thing was for certain: the person who killed Christopher was somebody staying in the same hotel that I was in, because every other person that was on that floor at the time of the shooting, every other person who surrounded Christopher's dead body, was Asian, so they would not know him at all, and therefore, the person who killed Christopher had to be somebody I had met the day before. I knew that my time had come to solve another baffling mystery.

Chapter 7

Whilst we descended from the tower, Chloe announced that she was taking everybody back to the hotel. Whilst we waited for the bus to pull up, something happened that astounded even me— Veronica broke down in hysterical sobs! She collapsed to the floor, holding her head in her hands and shouting, "I can't believe this has happened! Why did you take the man I love!"

Police cars were everywhere, as their owners tried to establish what had happened. However, I felt that it was my duty to do this investigation for a number of reasons. Firstly, the suspects would feel more comfortable talking to me, since I had already met them and conversed with them. Secondly, I felt that I was at a head start because I felt like I knew a lot about each of them already, and I had witnessed the events of that day. This murder was planned, so I was going to think back to see how everybody had behaved on the morning of that day. However, there was one other reason: I felt that I needed to solve this murder in order to redeem myself from the previous investigation. If I solved this murder, I would feel much more confident about going back to work, so I made it my own personal goal to solve this murder, as always.

And so, I decided to begin the investigation once we arrived back at the hotel.

On the way there, everyone on the bus talked about the murder and who could have done it, knowing fine well that the person who did do it was on board the bus. I was just sat there, thinking. Perhaps this person intended to murder two different people, and only hit Christopher? At this moment in time, it seemed like the main possibility.

We arrived back at the hotel, its ornate demeanor providing calm and comfort as though nothing terrible had happened that day. Firstly, I decided to interview the Sandersons, since they were closest to me, and for some reason, I was quite interested in talking to them anyway.

"Hello," I said, approaching them both.

"Are you investigating the murder?" said Shona.

Her straightforward question intrigued me, but I dismessed what she had said and moved on.

"Yes, I am investigating the murder, because that is what I do back home, and we owe this Cristopher, so I want to ask you just a couple of questions for now about the event that happened today," I replied.

"Are you a good detective?" asked Alan.

Again, I thought that was a rather unusual thing to say

"I'll be the one asking the questions, if you don't mind, Alan," I replied.

He apologized, and I started my investigation.

"So, where exactly were you when the first shot was heard?"

Shona decided to answer that question.

"Both of us were together, seeing to Stephanie. She was in such a state, poor thing!"

"Yes, I was there, too."

"So, that proves we did not do it!"

"Not exactly!" I said.

"How?" said Shona, looking confused. "You saw us when the shot was heard!"

"I saw you when the first shot was heard," I replied, "but not the second. I'm not accusing you of anything, just yet, but I am trying to keep my options open. Either one of you could have pulled a gun out and fired the gun at somebody else whilst we were distracted by the sight of Christopher. It looks like this could be a conspiracy, but I am not sure yet."

Both Alan and Shona seemed disappointed that they were not given alibis.

"So what was the point in asking us that question when you already knew the answer?" said Alan.

"I just wanted to see your reaction," was my reply. "There is another thing I would like to speak to you about."

"I think I know where this is going," said Alan.

"Yes," I replied, "well, last night, I did indeed see a woman kissing Christopher, and I overheard you two arguing about it, so I am assuming that the woman was you."

Shona looked ashamed of herself.

"It was only a fling," she said.

I felt upset for them. Ten years of marriage had been thrown away. I decided to end the chat there and move on to Stephanie and Brendan.

Like the Sandersons, I asked them where they were at the time of the first shot, and Stephanie replied, "Well, you saw me. I was on another side of the tower, crying on the ledge because I dropped an ice cream over the top."

Brendan said, "I was seeing to Stephanie. You saw me, didn't you?"

"Yes," I replied.

"Then why are you asking us these questions?"

"I wanted to see your reaction," was my reply, for the second time.

I knew that I was finished there, because Brendan and Stephanie had no apparent motive to murder.

After having interviewed those four suspects, I came to some sort of conclusion. Although I knew everything that was going to be said, that interview helped me; those four suspects looked calm and collected. That was quite strange, although it was not impossible for a murderer to act in that way.

I decided to focus on the first shot for now. Although I had seen Alan, Brendan, and Shona just before the shot was fired, it did not exclude them from the investigation, because they could have actually fired the first shot, knowing the structure of the Eiffel Tower. The only person who could not possibly have fired the first shot was Stephanie, because I saw her hands whilst the shot was fired.

I decided that it was probably not Alan, Brendan, or Shona, because they were still behind me, talking, and the shot seemed to come from a distance, making it unlikely that it was either of them. That left me with four possible shooters: Chloe, Veronica, Frank, or Doreen, all of whom I intended to interview. Now, I was getting to do some detective work.

Chapter 8

Veronica seemed to be calm now, so I decided to interview her next. When I saw her, she seemed to be lost in the surroundings as she sat in the seating area outside, sipping a glass of Death in the Afternoon; which confused and worried me, since she had confessed that she did not like that particular drink the night before.

"Hello, Veronica," I said, approaching her the way a mouse approaches a lion.

"Come to interview me, then, have you?" she said, not even looking at me.

"Yes," I replied, "you're alright with that, aren't you?"

"Well, I'd best get this over with, and I'll enjoy the rest of my holiday," she replied, still not looking at me.

That shocked me, what she had just said there. She showed no sympathy, or emotion, about what had happened.

"I'm sorry, do you remember what happened today?" I asked her.

"Yes. My husband was murdered. Next question," came Veronica's curt reply.

"You don't seem to care," I said.

"Well, my husband was a horrible man. I'm glad he's dead," she said, still gazing at the distant countryside.

"That makes me suspicious, you know," I added.

"I don't care if you think I did it or not. I did not shoot Christopher, so I have nothing to worry about."

"You might know that, but I don't, so I still need to speak to you," I said, getting frustrated with this woman. "I need to establish exactly where you were at the time of the first shot."

"I was on one side of the tower, looking out of it. That's what you do when you go up the Eiffel Tower, isn't it?" she said, getting more and more irritated by the minute.

"Did anybody see you at this time?"

"No. Nobody likes me. I tried socializing with the rest of them earlier on, but it didn't work well. I don't mix with people, and they don't mix with me, so, no. Nobody else was on that side of the tower at the time of the shooting."

"And what side of the tower was this?"

"Well, it was directly opposite you lot when that stupid girl screamed for dropping her ice cream; so it was at a right angle to Christopher. It's funny, isn't it? The four sides of the tower symbolize society. The side that I was on represents the lonely old women; the side that Christopher was on represents the lonely old men; the side that you lot were on represents the happy people, who have not a care in the world, and the other side represents the rest of us."

That made me think. My parents were on 'the other side'. I wondered what she meant by that. Perhaps she was being cryptic.

"You didn't see the Miltons, or Chloe?" I asked her.

"No. I am assuming that they were on the other side."

That assumption was for me to make. I left it there, since at this stage in the investigation, I had nothing else to ask her. She took one big gulp out of her glass, finishing it off, and then went and dived into the swimming pool, creating a big splash.

I found the Miltons, and looked forward, somewhat, to talking with them; they seemed like such a nice couple.

"Hello, dear," said Doreen, as I approached them. "How's the investigation coming along?"

"I'm just establishing exactly where everybody was at the time of the shooting," I said.

"Terrible business, isn't it?" said Frank, looking rather intrigued by the whole thing.

"Yes. So, would you mind telling me where the pair of you were when you heard the first shot?" I asked them.

"Well," said Doreen, "we had just gotten to the top of the last flight of stairs, and Chloe offered us a drink.

She had several bottles, just in case anyone wanted any. She had forgotten to tell all of us about it."

I sighed in my head. Silly Chloe, I thought.

"Anyway," Doreen continued, "we accepted her offer for a drink, so there was no need to stand in the long queue. We walked around for about thirty seconds, and then we heard a woman screaming. I think it was that young Stephanie. Anyway, we looked around the corner to see what was going on, and that was when we heard the shot, so we rushed over to the opposite side of the tower, and there he was—dead as a door nail!"

"Did you see Chloe, by any chance, when the shot was fired?" I asked them both.

Both of them shook their heads.

"We did not see her when the shot was fired, but she was with us when it happened. She stood next to us. One second later, we saw her rush over there with us."

"That's interesting," I said.

"So, did you know the Dewells well?" I asked them.

Again, both Frank and Doreen shook their heads. "We only met them yesterday," he said, "and I hope we don't see that woman again! She sounds insane!"

"You're not the only one who thinks that," I laughed.

I stopped the interview there, because I was quite eager to move on to Chloe. Chloe interested me; she seemed perfectly capable of committing a murder, and she certainly had the motive and opportunity, so she was at the top of my suspect list. It would not be fair to assume that she was indeed the murderer, because I had no proof that she was, but something about her just struck me as odd.

I found her, and, as usual, she rushed around trying to placate everyone with drinks and appetizers.

"Hello," Chloe said, "are you any closer to finding the person who did this ghastly thing?"

"I'm taking baby steps," I said, careful not to give any information away. "I need to talk to you next."

"Alright," replied Chloe, "but please make it quick. I have a business to run."

"So, where were you at the time of the first shooting?" I asked her.

"Well, I was on the opposite side of the tower as Christopher was," came her quick reply.

"Did anyone else see you there?"

"No. I don't think so, anyway. Everyone was too busy with the distraction of the shooting, including me. I can't really remember much, actually." Whilst she spoke, Chloe wrote down calculations on a piece of paper.

"Did you see anything else that we can regard as suspicious?"

"No," said Chloe, who only seemed half-interested by what I had to say.

"Did you see the Miltons when you heard the shot?"

"No...wait. Yes, I did. I was with them, and they were right next to me, so they could not have done it. Anyway, they wouldn't do such a thing."

"I think it's fair to say you had it in for Veronica and Christopher?"

Chloe just looked at me.

"I did not do this, you know," said Chloe.

"I am not assuming anything at the moment," I said, trying to reassure her, "but it seems to me that you are one of the few suspects who do not have a valid alibi."

"What? There were plenty of people on the same side as me! How could I have done it when everybody was surrounding me?!"

"The same way in which the person with the gun placed it under my seat whilst I, and everybody else, were distracted. I am not saying that you are the murderer, and I am not accusing you of anything, but I cannot rule you out!"

"So, who do you think did it, then?" Chloe asked, much calmer now.

"I don't know for certain, like I just said," I replied.

"Well, if there is anything..."

"Yeah. I'll ask."

"And don't forget to enjoy your holiday!" Chloe said with a smile. "You have to remember, you're still on holiday. You need to relax!"

Although it seemed like Chloe was trying to drive me away from investigating the murder, what she was saying was true. I did need to relax, although that was not going to happen now. I needed to regain my energy before going back to work. In fact, I had not thought of work once after the day before, because I was having so much fun and was distracted. I just wanted to get the murder solved and over with before moving on with my life back at home.

Chapter 9

I decided to relax for a while, to see if that got me anywhere. Having established where everybody was at the time of the murder, I decided to think back to the events of the day. It had been one of the most dramatic days of my life, because so much had happened in the space of twenty-four hours. I thought and thought, just like I always did when it came to solving a case.

Soon, I realized that it was not going to get me anywhere, so I wrote down all of the suspects, and crossed out the people who could not have fired the first shot. I knew that Stephanie did not, because she was physically there when I heard it fired. Chloe had excluded the Miltons from the investigation with her statement, so it was certainly not them. That left me with five potential murderers, and any one of them could have done it.

It did cross my mind that this was some sort of conspiracy between two people, although I was not certain of which two. Indeed, it could have just been one person.

I then sat back and thought about the nature of the crime. Perhaps the tower itself symbolized something? I thought, out of all the places in the world, why pick the Eiffel Tower to commit murder? In my mind, the Eiffel Tower represented love, and it probably did to most people. At the heart of Paris, I viewed the Eiffel Tower as the most romantic place in the world, so I decided that love was most probably involved with the killing.

That gave a big hint as to who the murderer was, although it still could have been several people. I did not want to cross them out just yet. I could not help but think that Alan and Shona were indeed innocent. Although they were behind me when the shot was fired, so they could have done it, though I'm not sure how. However, the shot seemed to have come from a distance. It was a huge shame that I could not tell exactly where it had come from.

I then moved on to the second shot, and why that might have been fired. There was a number of reasons. Firstly, it could have been fired to kill someone, so this may have been planned to be a double murder. It could have also been fired as a distraction technique. Was I supposed to think that this was planned as a double killing? If that was the case, it simply could have been fired by accident.

Sticking to the subject of the second shot, I thought more about who could have done that. Again, I wrote down all of the suspects who were in my sight when the second shot was fired. I went around to every guest and asked each of them one question: who did you see when the second shot was fired?

I wrote down everything they told me:

Frank saw both Doreen and Shona because they stood next to him. Doreen saw Frank and Brendan. Brendan saw Veronica, Stephanie, Shona and Alan. Stephanie saw, Brendan, Shona, Veronica and Alan. Shona saw Alan and Veronica. Alan saw Shona, Stephanie and Veronica. Chloe saw Shona, Stephanie and Brendan. Veronica saw nobody: she was simply lost in staring at her dead husband.

As I analyzed these findings, I came to the conclusion through witness statements that the potential murderers were Chloe, Frank and Doreen. However, as I thought more about it, it might not have necessarily been true, because some people may have been mistaken and some may have even been lying. Assuming that everybody told the truth, Veronica, Shona, Alan, Stephanie and Brendan were seen by at least three different people, so it was most likely that they did not fire the second shot. This became more and more puzzling by the minute, but I knew that I could solve it, so I continued.

As I was lost in my trail of thought, Chloe approached me, telling me that the police wanted to see me.

Fortunately, they spoke English, so I did not need Chloe to act as a translator.

"We understand that you are investigating the murder that was committed on the Eiffel Tower earlier today?" one of the policemen asked.

"Yes, I am," I replied.

"Well, we would just like to inform you that the gun used to murder Christopher Dewell has been found, and there were no fingerprints on it."

"Where was it?" I asked.

"It was lodged in between two iron bars, so it must have been thrown out somehow."

I thanked the police, and sat back down. Chloe offered me another Death in the Afternoon, but I refused, asking for some orange juice instead. With that new information, I decided to think just a little bit more.

Chapter 10

I could not help but think that Chloe was the one who did this. I was never one to be judgmental of another, and I never, ever assumed anything in this job, but I just had that feeling that she was the murderer. I had to admit, although I had solved perhaps some of the most complex cases in the country, I was still an inexperienced amateur.

Before I went to France, I had solved only four cases (excluding the one that I solved but justice was not brought to the murderer), so I had little experience in these types of cases. Of course, I had solved countless amounts of gang killings, which aided me some, but it was only rare that I had come across a case where ordinary people were the culprit.

I knew that the murderer was under the very roof that I was under, but I just could not see it. Other detectives work in a way where they look at someone and suspect them, and then start to follow them and gather evidence on them, but I did not like to work in that way. My method of solving cases is to suspect everyone, and only assume who the murderer is when there is no doubt whatsoever that they did it.

Then, a dark thought came into my mind: will the murderer strike again? It was possible, since there could have been a targeted second victim, so it was a possibility (if not, probability) that the murderer would strike again, meaning that anybody could be in danger!

For now, I decided to watch Chloe very carefully, despite my opinions of this technique. I knew it was the only way to move forward for now. Chloe was the usual business woman, stressed, trying to be kind, well organized, professionally dressed, and tough on the inside and outside. If she was indeed the killer, she would be a tough nut to crack. I wished that there would be some sort of evidence to exclude her from the inquiries, but unfortunately, I did not think that it could happen.

Chloe could have easily committed the murder; she had the motive, because she despised the Dewells. Perhaps she hoped to have Veronica arrested for the crime. She also had the opportunity to murder Christopher; she knew the Eiffel Tower inside and our, so it was fair to say that she knew where every iron bar was, and at what angle she could shoot Christopher from. She also had the means to do it. she was both physically and mentally capable of firing a gun at somebody and killing them. In a court of law, you need motive, opportunity, and means. Chloe had all three. That is why I suspected her.

So there I was, deciding to stalk Chloe in order to analyze her behavior, to see if she would slip up.

Chloe was at the reception, checking on another couple.

"Hello, and welcome to the Sunshine Hotel!" she said, as if she was a broken record, carrying on as if nothing had happened. She checked in this couple the same way as she checked in my family. It was like she had truly forgotten about the murder!

"Any developments yet?" she asked when she saw me, rubbing her hands together.

"Not quite," I said, "but I know I'm getting close."

"Oh...right," was Chloe's reply. Her head shook as if she had been threatened by me or something. Perhaps she had been.

I stayed in the reception room, and listened to her enter the kitchen. She started to shout at the cooks in French in an aggressive manner I had never witnessed coming from her.

She stormed out of the kitchen and went into the seating area where the Miltons were.

"Would you like another drink?" she asked them, in an overly polite and friendly manner.

I continued this for a while, watching and listening to her every move, the suspicion still there. I figured that she would become know my suspicions if I continued following her, so I decided to give it a rest for a while. Everything that she did for that twenty minutes was completely normal, which in itself would be abnormal considering the circumstances. I would assume that any innocent person would be respectful towards Christopher, but then again, this was Chloe I was thinking about. Perhaps it was Chloe's way. After all, she did have a business to run.

I went out the back, where I found my mother, looking out at the view.

"Your poor father's sunburned," she said, "so he's just gone to lie down for a while."

"That's a shame," I replied, "but let's not let it ruin our holiday."

"Tammy, if a murder is not going to ruin our holiday, then a little sunburn won't," my mother said, chuckling.

"That's true," I agreed.

"So, are you any further along?"

"I am still on the first day, remember? These things do take time."

"I know. Who do you have in mind as the killer?"

"Well, I can't help, but think it's Chloe."

"Chloe? No. It can't be!"

"Why do you think that?" I asked.

"Because I saw her when the shot was fired."

"You what?!" I cried.

"Joe and I were on the same ledge as Chloe and the Miltons. I saw Chloe standing right next to the ledge when the shot was fired."

"Are you sure?" I said, astounded.

"I am certain. I don't know where the shot came from, but it could not have been Chloe."

"Why didn't you mention this earlier?"

"Well, I thought I'd save it until you questioned me!"

In all of the drama, I had forgotten to question my own parents! It would have saved me a lot of time if I had.

"Well, this changes everything!" I said, knowing that I would have to start again.

"Yes..." my mother said. "Anyway, how are you and Danny?" she said, trying to change the conversation.

"Still separated," I replied, hinting that I did not want to talk about it.

"I was devastated when you broke up with him," my mother said, interfering with my life as usual.

"He's not the one for me," I said, "he stalks me. It's creepy."

"He stalks you because he cares about you. He made a mistake. Your father and I made a mistake, didn't we? When things got stressful, we separated, and then got back together again."

"But that was different. Your mother had just been murdered."

"And you were moving out. You got involved with that Alesha Christen case, and perhaps he did not like it. It's worth thinking about."

Later that night, after another think about the events of that day, I picked up my phone.

"Danny?" I said, "is that you?"

"Tammy?" Danny said on the other end of the line. "It's been so long. I can't believe I'm hearing your voice again."

"Well, you have. Why don't we meet up next week?"

"I'd love to."

I felt a lot better after that. Perhaps deep down, he was the one, and I did care for him. My life was crushed when he broke up with me, but now, perhaps we were going to pick up the pieces and start afresh. But for now, I still had a case to focus on.

Chapter 11

I thought, as usual. I thought and thought. After a long while, I decided that it was no use thinking about the first and second shots, so I decided to focus my attention on the gun that was found on the boat. How did it get there, and is there a link to the murder?

I tried to remember where everybody was, and what they were doing at the time of the murder. I remembered where everybody sat: the Sandersons and Brendan were behind me, Stephanie was right in front of me, taking a photo, Veronica was behind us, talking to the Miltons, and Chloe was there, doing whatever she was doing. Then, it came to me. I knew who the murderer was. One person out of that bunch was doing something else, and that person did what they did for a different purpose. I now knew who fired the first shot, and who fired the second shot. The whole thing had come together. This was a very cleverly planned murder, but it still did not defeat me.

I went downstairs to make the announcement that I had solved the murder.

"Hello, Tammy," said Chloe. "How are you getting on with the investigation."

"I have solved it!" I cried.

"You mean, you know who did it already?" she said with a very puzzled look.

"Oh, yes," I said, rather smug but also very confident.

"Who is it then?" she asked.

"I will explain everything when everybody is together. Could you do that for me?" I asked Chloe.

"Of course. Come on, give me a clue!"

"Alright then. I will give you several. Consider the following things: the structure of the hotel, the structure of the tower, the boat ride, the stairs of the tower, an ice cream, the red seating area, and the swimming pool. Given all of that information, you should be able to link each one together and then work out who killed Christopher Dewell."

Chloe just stared at me. "I think it would be best if you just explained it to me," she said, rushing off to get the guests.

Chapter 12

As usual, all of the suspects were gathered around the room, waiting for my denouncement.

"Well, then," I said, "it's time a few confessions are made, isn't it?"

I looked around the room, knowing who the killer was and glanced at this person.

"I really don't know where to start on this one, to be honest," I said, looking at the police in the background. "I think I know where to start. I know for a fact that this was indeed a conspiracy!"

Shocked faces roamed the room, glancing from one to another.

"Yes, it was. I had already established where everybody was at the time of the first shooting, and where everybody apparently was at the time of the second shot. This gave me a clue as to who was involved in this conspiracy. These conspirators almost got away with it, managing to discuss their crime right under my nose, and I did not notice. When I look back at it, I now realize how stupid I have been. Five people are involved.

"Before I announce who the conspirators are, I would like to take you to the night before the murder, or last night, at this cocktail party. When I went outside for some air, I was quite astounded to see Christopher Dewell kissing another woman. I automatically assumed that he was kissing Shona. However, I now know that Christopher was, in fact, kissing Stephanie."

"What?!" cried a horrified Stephanie, "how did you work that one out?"

"It was easy, Stephanie, although I did not directly see you, I heard the woman say that nobody had seen her. If this had been Shona, or even Chloe, then that would not have been the case, because Shona had informed Alan that she was going out for some air. Therefore, somebody had seen her leave the building. You, on the other hand, could have easily left the building, because everybody was so focused on Veronica Dewell; and because Brendan is so sociable and friendly, you were able to slip out for a few minutes."

"So you think I'm the killer?" she said.

"I did not say that," I replied, "but Brendan found out, didn't he?"

"What are you talking about?" she said, glancing at Brendan.

"Brendan found out about it. I don't know how, but he did. I assume he did see you when you came back. Both you and Brendan wanted to save your marriage, and you were determined not to let him wreck your lives. When you went back to the apartment that night, you overheard the Sandersons arguing about Shona's affair with Christopher.

"That was when the light bulb went off in your head. Knowing that Veronica also hated Christopher Dewell, you arranged to meet somewhere to discuss this event, and decided to meet in the morning, because that would be when everybody else was busy getting ready for the day's guided tour; so you would not attract any attention.

"Stephanie invited me up to her room to help her look for some sun cream. However, that was a lie, because the only reason she went up there was to change the red towel from her balcony to a blue towel. Veronica, Brendan, and the Sandersons were all in the red seating area, which is directly below Stephanie's room, and when they saw the blue towel, they obeyed the signal and changed to the swimming pool area. This is because my parents and Chloe were all around the reception, which is right next to the seating area. Stephanie knew that the swimming pool would be more private, so you could all discuss your plans there.

"Now, when you went on the boat ride, you all had a part to play. Stephanie offered to take a photograph of my parents and I, which we naturally accepted thus distracting us. Veronica played her part by talking to Chloe and the Miltons, keeping them focused on her. While everybody was preoccupied, either Alan, or

Shona, slipped the gun next to me. I think that this was because I needed something else to focus on, or perhaps it was because Chloe was always getting up, running around everywhere, like she always did. They may have wanted me to think it was them."

I looked around again, waiting for a response.

"Is that all you have on us?" asked Stephanie.

"Oh, no," I said, "I haven't even gotten to the tower part yet. When we got to the Eiffel Tower, Chloe offered the Miltons to stay behind so they could take their time. I stayed as well. This gave the rest of the conspirators a chance to dash up the stairs, and sort out last minute details, including buying the ice cream. Stephanie walked past me with her ice cream, making certain that I had seen it, and dropped it over the edge, thus creating a diversion and an alibi for the four of them.

"While we all focused on Stephanie, Veronica picked up the gun she had concealed in her pocket, and shot Christopher. She was able to do this because of the structure of the floor of the tower. When the shot was fired, everybody ran over to him, and Veronica took her time, making sure she was not the first to get there. While everybody was distracted, she handed the gun to Alan, who fired it in the air, producing the second shot. The whole purpose of doing this was to give Veronica an alibi.

"However, I did not see her when the second shot was fired, so this failed slightly, but this did not matter, because three of the conspirators said that they saw her when the shot was fired. In addition, they each gave each other alibis, which would push me towards Chloe and the Miltons."

Silence filled the room.

"Well, Tammy, I'm afraid you're wrong. You have no evidence that we did it."

It was true. I had no evidence. My stomach churned. I did not want a repeat of the previous case, but I needn't have worried.

"Oh, shut up, Veronica!" cried Shona, "we all know you did it!"

"What?!" cried Veronica.

"You're right, Tammy," said Shona, "I admit, I made a terrible, terrible, mistake, and I deserve to be punished. Everything you said there was one hundred percent correct!"

Shona broke down.

"How could you?" Alan said, moving away from his wife, feeling deserted.

"And you're not innocent, either! I hate you for forcing me into this! And you Veronica, I don't care if I go to prison for ten years, I hate you. You're an evil bitch!"

"How dare you!" screamed Veronica.

"I know about you and Alan, so there's no point in denying it!"

Brendan and Stephanie just sat there, their faces pale, knowing it was over for them.

The police had heard enough and took all five of them away, never to be seen by me again.

After things had settled down, my parents and I enjoyed the rest of our holiday, although I felt rather alone now that most everybody had gone. Still, we had the Miltons to talk to, and we enjoyed our conversations with them.

I did receive a shock on the last day, when Chloe said to me, "I've been thinking, Tammy. Since you solved the murder earlier this week, I would like to offer you a free holiday for next year! Oh, and since the Miltons have had to put up with this as well, they can come, too!"

I never thought Chloe would be this charitable, but I accepted the offer. However, the free holiday was not the main reward. The main reward for me was getting back on my feet again. I was now more motivated than ever to get on with my work, and more confident than ever to catch killers, and bring them down once and for all.

I returned to the UK, where I was happy to see my boss, though he did not reciprocate my elatedness.

"Tammy, I've got some bad news for you," he said.

"What is it?" I asked.

"You had a boyfriend, Danny?"

"Yes?" I replied, wondering where he was because he did not pick up his phone when I arrived back in England.

"Well, yesterday, Danny was killed in a car accident."

My knees went weak. "How?" I whispered, still not believing the news.

Someone ran a red light and t-boned his car. He was killed instantly," said my boss, trying to sound sympathetic, but failing. "I'm…I'm sorry. Why don't you take the rest of the week off."

He motioned for an officer to walk me to my car, making certain I got there all right. I still couldn't believe it. Despite all of the pain he had caused me, I never wanted this. After regaining my confidence in my ability to solve a murder, after finally relaxing and regaining my belief in myself, all of that was ripped from me once again. I started my car and drove home in a daze, wondering how I would deal with the aftermath of Danny's passing.

About the Author

Brie Krauss lives in the United States with her family. Though not planning on becoming a writer, she had a few murder mysteries rolling around in her head and decided to write them on day, mostly so she could stop thinking about them. Always a fan of novellas, and quick entertainment, she kept the Closed Case stories short on purpose and hopes you enjoy them.

More by Brie Kraus

Closed Case

Curious Confession
Over the Hills
Murder on the Eiffel Tower
Unfinished Business

Other Books

Don't Ask
I Hate You Rock Stars